It was BIG It was SCARY It was . . .

The Elf A. Bits Series

Diana Trenda Aubut

Leslie Cannella Nordness

Our books are written in honor of our children
Levi, Logan, Luc, Ryan
Jessica, Tommi, Victoria, Bethany

A portion of the proceeds from this book will be donated to charities for children.

River City Kids
an imprint of River City Publishing

This Book
Belongs to

The Elf A. Bits™

The Elf A. Bits / The Original Find N. Elf (c) 2001

The Elf A. Bits love to play Hide Them, Find Them every day!

A. Lil Elf
B. Anne Elf
C. Dee Elf
D. Tiny Elf
E. Kan Elf
F. Everan Elf
G. Whiz Elf
H. Youan Elf
I. Amyour Elf
J. Ammin Elf
K. Nine Elf
L. Vis Elf
M. Tooan Elf

N. Awesome Elf
O. Myan Elf
P. King Elf
Q. Tea Elf
R. Uan Elf
S. Datan Elf
T. Knee Elf
U. Noah Elf
V. My Elf
W. WWDotcom Elf
X. Cellent Elf
Y. Notan Elf
Z. Baby Elf

5 GAMES
100 PIECES
PUZZLES

There was a monster under my bed,
it was big, it was scary,
it was **RED**.

My Dad chased it away,
but it came back
the very next day.

This monster was really mean,
it was big, it was scary,
it was GREEN.

5 GAMES
100 PIECES
2 PUZZLES
once upon a time
There was a little

One day Mom said,
"U. Noah Elf
lives behind the books
on your shelf."

I said, "Oh, I really don't think
he can get rid of a monster
that is big, that is scary,
that is **PINK**.

FAIRY TALE
There is no
such things as monsters mom
NUBERS
CATS
5 GAMES
7 PUZZLES

An Elf popped out
from behind a book
and said, "Let me take a look."

He said, "Don't worry, little fellow,
I'll get rid of that monster even if
it is big, and scary, and ."

U. Noah said, "I'm going under there."

I said, " You better beware."

He said, "Oh, I have a way

of getting rid of monsters

that are big, that are scary,

that are **GRAY**."

3 GAMES
100 PIECES
PUZZLES

There was a lot of noise,

and it lasted all day.

But all those monsters

did go away.

U. Noah found my shoes and my shirt.

Some socks, some toys, and a little bit of dirt.

U. Noah kicked it right out the door
and said, "Don't worry, it won't bother you any more."

That monster got right out of town.
it was big, it was scary
it was **BROWN.**

BLOCKS
5 GAMES
100 PIECES
2PUZZLES

Now U. Noah Elf sleeps in my bed too.

Just in case
there are monsters
who are big, who are scary,
who are **BLUE.**

THE END!

THE ELF A. BITS™

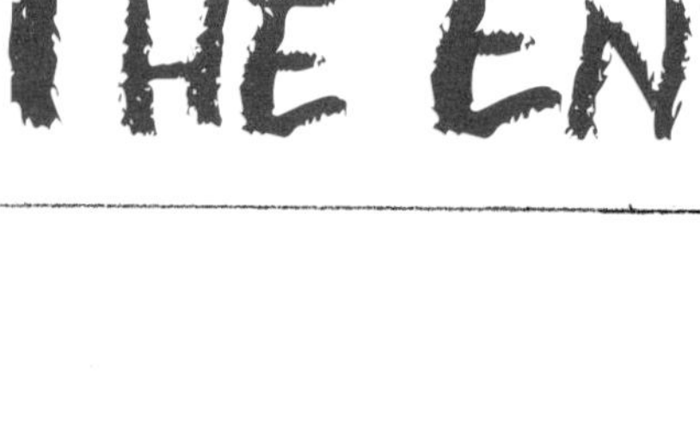

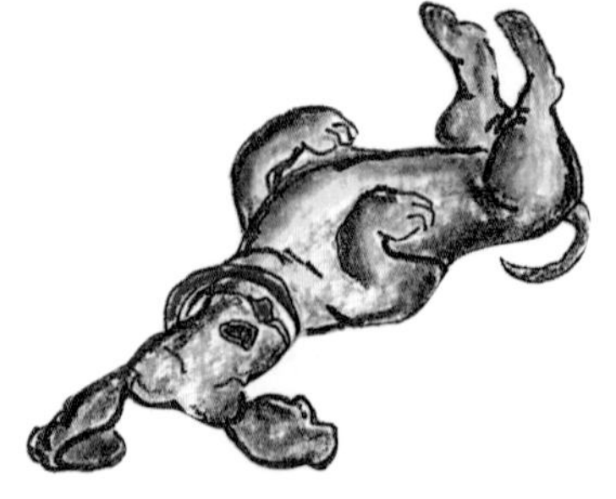

The Original Find N. Elf series
is an interactive concept
for children and adults.
HIDE them in fun places
for your family to SEEK.

Please e-mail us at
THEELFABITS@AOL.COM
with your HIDE and SEEK stories.
We know your family
will love this game as much
as our family does.
Have fun
with your Elf A. Bits.

About Diana and Leslie

Diana and Leslie consider their partnership to be divine intervention—a hug from God! Their perfect partnership began with eight children between them, an artistic background, and shared enthusiasm about the wonders of childhood.

Diana, who lived in Louisiana for many years, now resides in Birmingham, Alabama, with her husband Mitch and their children Levi, Logan, Tommi, and Luc. Her oldest daughter, Jessica, lives in Birmingham with her husband Mike and son Jakob. Diana's creativity as a sculptor and writer inspired the Elf-A-Bits series.

Leslie, born and raised in Louisiana, currently resides in Birmingham with her husband Steve and children Ryan and Victoria. Daughter Bethany will attend college in the fall. Besides writing and sculpting, Leslie loves her dog and birds, and enjoys reading, playing tennis, and working in her garden.

Diana and Leslie now bring the Elf-A-Bits series to create family traditions for children throughout the world. They encourage you to share the magic with your family.